The Magician of Puddle Lane

and other stories

Produced by Allegra Publishing Ltd, London
for Mercury Books Ltd
Editor : Felicia Law
Designer : Karen Radford

Published by
Mercury Junior an imprint of Mercury Books
20 Bloomsbury Street
London WC1B 3JH, UK

ISBN 978 1845600402

The Magician of Puddle Lane

and other stories

Sheila McCullagh

Illustrated by
Prue Theobalds, Tony Morris, Gavin Rowe,
John Dillow, Bookmatrix, India

Mercury Junior

Puddle Lane looked like any other street and its inhabitants were quite ordinary too. In fact, everything was quite normal - except for one thing! The Magician!

The Magician lived in an attic room in the old house in Puddle Lane. He didn't often go down into the lane, but he had a magic puddle of water on the floor of his room. When he looked into the puddle and said the right spell, the water in the magic puddle became as clear as glass. He could look into it and see what was happening down below in Puddle Lane.

Sometimes he left presents for the children in his garden. And sometimes – he just had to use his magic to put things right …

The Magic Box

The Magician would have been very lonely if there had been no children living in the lane too. He liked children and he didn't mind a bit if they played in his garden. He always left the gate open to welcome them in.

He soon made friends with the children in Puddle Lane – Sarah and Davy, Hari and Gita.

One day, Sarah was outside
in Puddle Lane. Sarah and
Davy had made a wooden
cart but one of the wheels
had fallen off.

Sarah was just putting
the wheel back on again
when she looked up and
saw Mrs Pitter-Patter.

Mrs Pitter-Patter who lived in Puddle Lane
was always asking questions.

The children who lived in the lane
did their best to be polite to her,
but they found her a nuisance
just the same. (So did their parents!)

"Sarah!" cried Mrs Pitter-Patter.
"Whatever are you doing?
You'll make your dress all
dirty, and your mother will
be very angry with you!"

9

"No, she won't, Mrs Pitter-Patter," said Sarah.
"She knows all about it. I've got my old clothes
on. It's my birthday, and the Magician said that
he would leave a present in the garden for me.
He said it was a big one, so I'm taking my
cart to carry it home."

"You'll tear your clothes on the
bushes," cried Mrs Pitter-Patter.
"Surely your mother doesn't let
you play in the Magician's garden!"

"Yes, she does," said Sarah.
"She knows the Magician.
He's a friend of ours.
It's a lovely place to play."

Just then Davy came along the lane.
He had a rope in his hand.
There were two big knobs at one
end of the cart.
Davy and Sarah tied the ends
of the rope to the knobs.

Mrs Pitter-Patter watched them
with a frown. "That's the wrong
way to tie it," she said.

"We always tie it this way,
Mrs Pitter-Patter," said Davy.

Mrs Pitter-Patter shook
her head and went back
down Puddle Lane,
muttering to herself.

Davy checked the back wheel.
Then he pushed the garden gates open
and Sarah pulled the cart through.
The rope worked very well,
and Davy shut the gates.

"Where has the Magician
left your present?" he asked.

Sarah looked all around,
to see if she could see it.

She saw a big box by the hollow tree.
"There it is! Look!" she cried.
She ran over to the tree.
The box was wrapped in red paper
and tied with the golden ribbon.
A big white card was propped
up against it.

"It's got my name on it,"
she said.

SARAH

Sarah was right. Her
name was written on
the card in big letters.

"What is in the box?" asked Davy,
running across to the tree.

"How do I know till I've opened
it?" said Sarah. "I'll open it now."

She took off the ribbon and
pulled off the paper and
uncovered a beautiful box.
Sarah sat looking at it for
a moment or two.

The box was painted blue
and gold and there was
a big red button on the top.

"I wonder what's inside it?
And how do you open it?"

Davy picked up the card.
"Wait a minute," he said.
"There's something written on the
back of the card. Look! It says,
'Don't open the box.
Push the red button.'

"What good is a box if you
can't open it?" asked Sarah.

"It might be a magic box,"
said Davy. "You'd better do
what the Magician says."

"All right," said Sarah.
"I'll try it."
She pushed the red button.

15

At once, the box began
to play a tune. Sarah felt
her feet begin to dance.
She couldn't stop them.
The tune was a dancing
tune and her feet
danced with it.

Davy was dancing too.
He couldn't help it. They
joined hands and danced
around and around until
the music stopped.

"It's a music box!" cried Sarah. (She was
out of breath.) "What a lovely present!"
"It's a magic music box," said Davy.
"I couldn't stop dancing."

"Neither could I," said Sarah.
"My feet wouldn't stop.
Let's take the box back
to Puddle Lane."

They lifted the box
into the cart and pulled
it back carefully to the
garden gates.

When they got Puddle Lane they saw Mr Gotobed.
Mr Gotobed lived in the house next to the Magician's
garden. He spent most of the day
in bed, sleeping. But sometimes
he took his chair outside into
the lane and went to sleep
in the sunshine. He was fast
asleep now, sitting in his chair.

Sarah looked at Davy.
"I'm going to push the button and
see what happens!" she whispered.
She pushed the red button.

18

At once the music box began to play.
Old Mr Gotobed woke up with a start. He jumped out of
his chair and began to dance. Sarah and Davy joined hands
and danced around until the music stopped.

"Well!" cried Mr Gotobed,
as he sat down in his chair
again. "Well, well, well! I haven't
danced liked that since I was
a boy. That's a wonderful
music box, Sarah!"

"It's my birthday today," said Sarah.
"It was a present from the Magician."

"A present from the Magician!"
said Mr Gotobed. "That explains it.
It's a magic music box."

Mrs Pitter-Patter came pattering
back up the lane. She saw the box.
"What have you got there, Sarah?" she cried.
"It's my birthday present from the Magician," said Sarah.
"Nonsense!" cried Mrs Pitter-Patter. "The Magician
would never give you a beautiful box like that!
You must put it back where you found it.
And what's that button?"

"Don't touch it,
Mrs Pitter-Patter!"
cried Davy. "It's
a magic box."

"Of course I'll touch
it if I want to," said
Mrs Pitter-Patter.
And she pressed
the red button.

This time the box didn't play its
dancing tune. It began to sing:

'Mrs Pitter Patter,
patters up the lane.
Mrs Pitter-Patter,
patters home again.
Mrs Pitter-Patter,
telling people what to do.
Pitter-patter, clitter-clatter,
chitter-chatter-choo!'

As soon as the box began to sing,
Mrs Pitter-Patter's feet began to dance.
She twirled around and around in the lane.
"Oh!" cried Mrs Pitter-Patter. "Oh! Whatever is it?
Whatever is happening to me?"
On and on she danced, right up Puddle Lane.

Mrs Pitter-Patter was the only one who was dancing.
Sarah and Davy and Mr Gotobed stood watching
her dance, until at last the box stopped singing and
Mrs Pitter-Patter went in the door of her own house.

"I hope she's all right," said Davy. "She was
dancing very fast."
"Oh, she'll be all right," said Mr Gotobed.
It's very happy music. I don't think it
could hurt her. I enjoyed my dance.
But you'd better take that box
home with you now, Sarah.
I'm worn out, and
I'm going to take
a little nap."

Mr Gotobed sat down in his chair.
He put his handkerchief over his
head and went back to sleep.
As the children watched,
he began to snore gently.

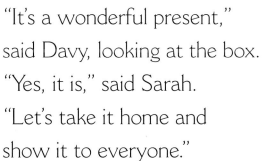

"It's a wonderful present,"
said Davy, looking at the box.
"Yes, it is," said Sarah.
"Let's take it home and
show it to everyone."

So Sarah and Davy
took the magic music
box home.

The Magic Balloons

One day, the Magician looked
into his magic puddle of water to
see what was going on in Puddle
Lane. He saw old Mr Gotobed
sitting outside his house
in the lane.

Mr Gotobed was sitting
in the afternoon sunshine,
and he was fast asleep.

Puddle Lane was very quiet and peaceful. It was the perfect place to take a nap. Mr Gotobed had settled down to sleep for the whole afternoon.

But just then, the quiet was broken. Peter Puffle came charging up the lane, riding his wagon.
He had a tin trumpet in his hand and he blew the trumpet loudly in Mr Gotobed's ear as he went by.

Mr Gotobed woke up with a start,
but before he could say anything,
Peter had turned his wagon
around and charged off
down the lane.

Mr Gotobed nearly
fell out of his chair.
"I wish that boy would
play somewhere else!"
he said.

He got up and
went into his house,
shaking his head.

Sarah and Davy came through the gates out of
the garden. They were pulling their music box
along on the old cart they had
made. Peter came rushing
back up the lane on
his wagon.

"Hello, Peter," said Davy.
"Let's have a blow on
that trumpet."
"Get one for yourself.
This one's mine," said Peter.

He turned his wagon round
and went off down the lane.

"Never mind, Davy," said Sarah.
"Our music box is much better
than his silly trumpet."

She gave the cart a pull,
but as it moved forward
the wheel fell off again.

"Now it won't move," said Sarah. "We'll have to mend it."
"It's the same wheel as last time," said Davy.
"We need a longer nail."

They lifted the magic music box
out of the cart and set it down
on the ground. Then they
turned the cart on one
side to look at
the wheel.

They were just trying to fix the wheel
on again, when Peter Puffle came
rushing back, riding his wagon.
He stopped to watch them.

"Huh!" he said. "Has that
old thing broken down again?
I don't think much of your cart!"

"Lend us your wagon, Peter,"
said Sarah. "Then we can take
the music box home and come
back for the cart."

31

"You can't have my wagon," said Peter.
"I need it."
"It will only be for a few minutes,
Peter," said Davy. "Just while
we take the music box home.
It's not far."
"Then you can carry it,"
said Peter. "It's my wagon,
and I'm playing with it."

And he went off
down the lane.

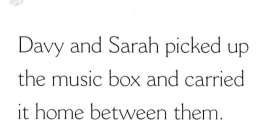

Davy and Sarah picked up
the music box and carried
it home between them.

The Magician had seen everything in his magic puddle of water.

"I think Peter Puffle needs to learn a lesson," he said. "I think I'll go down into Puddle Lane myself. I'll make a little magic and we'll see what happens then!"

He went to his magic book, muttered a spell, and snapped his fingers.

33

In a flash, the Magician vanished and an old
man stood there, with a bunch of balloons
in his hand. The Magician laughed softly
to himself and went out of his
attic room. He went down
the stairs and through
the garden and out
into Puddle Lane.

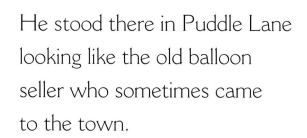

He stood there in Puddle Lane
looking like the old balloon
seller who sometimes came
to the town.

Peter Puffle came charging up the lane in his
wagon. He saw the Magician and stopped.

"Are you selling those balloons?"
he asked. "I'll have them."
"How many do you want?"
asked the Magician.
"I want them all," said Peter.
"Aren't there other children
in Puddle Lane who might
like one?" asked the Magician.
"Yes," said Peter. "But I'm
here first. I'll buy them all."

He pulled out his money
and the Magician gave him
the bunch of balloons.

As soon as Peter took hold of the bunch of balloons, he shot up into the air.

He hung there, as high as the roofs of the houses. He clung to the balloons as hard as he could.
"Help!" cried Peter.
"Help! Help! Get me down!"

Sarah and Davy came running out of
their house to see what was the matter.
"Peter!" cried Sarah. "Come down!"
"I can't come down," cried Peter. "Help!"

Hari and Gita looked out of their door.
"We'll get a ladder," cried Hari.

"There's no need for a ladder," said the Magician. "Let go of the balloons one by one. Remember, don't let them all go at once. If you let them go one at a time, you will come down slowly."

The Magician lifted one finger.
"Remember, Peter!
One at a time," he said

Peter let a balloon go and
he came down a little way
towards the ground.

"That's the way,"
said the Magician.

The beautiful yellow
balloon floated down
and Sarah caught it.

39

"Now let the next one go,"
said the Magician. "Remember -
one at a time!"

Peter let another balloon go, and
then another. He dropped down
until he could see into the top
windows of the houses.

The balloons floated down into
Puddle Lane. Gita caught one
and Hari caught the other one.

"Now another one," said the Magician,
"and then one more."

Peter let two more balloons go.
He dropped down even further.
A green balloon floated down
and Davy caught it.

"Now let all the others go,"
said the Magician.

Peter let the rest of the balloons go.
He dropped safely to the ground.
The balloons floated away, up and
over the roofs of the houses.

"Are you all right, Peter?" asked Davy.

"I think so," said Peter. "But it wasn't fair!
It was a trick."

"Here's your balloon," said Gita,
holding it out to him.

"You can have it," said Peter.
"I don't want it. I don't want
any of them. You can keep
the lot of them!"

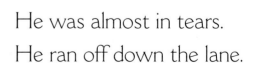

He was almost in tears.
He ran off down the lane.

Sarah turned to the Magician.

"What shall we do with the balloons?" she asked.

"Play with them," said the Magician.

"Can we really?" asked Gita.

"Of course you can," said the Magician.

"They're yours. Peter gave them to you."

The Magician turned around and went back up
the lane to his house, laughing softly. The children
stood watching him until he went into the garden.

"That was the Magician himself, wasn't it?"
asked Gita.

"It must have been," said Hari.
"And those must have been
magic balloons."

"They don't seem to be magic
now," said Davy. "I think
he wanted us to have them."

"Let's go and mend our cart,"
said Sarah. "And then we can
play with the balloons."

The four chilldren went
off up the lane together
to mend the old cart.

Mrs Pitter-Patter and the Magician

Mrs Pitter-Patter was always telling everyone else what they ought to do. Most people took no notice, but she still went on telling them.

One day she went out. The sun was shining and the sky was blue. She saw Miss Baker making bread, and told her that she ought to make a cake. Mrs Pitter-Patter went on up the lane, while Miss Baker just shook her head and put the bread in the oven.

She saw Mr Puffle. Mr Puffle was painting his door green, and she told him that he ought to paint it white. Mrs Pitter-Patter went on up the lane, and Mr Puffle just opened another can of green paint.

She saw Hari and Gita
Hari and Gita lived in Puddle
Lane. They were playing with
a ball. Mrs Pitter-Patter told
them that they ought to get
a jump rope instead.

"It's much better for you
to jump about," she said.
"And you mustn't play in the
lane. You should play in the
garden of the old house."

Mrs Pitter-Patter went
on up the lane, and Hari
threw the ball to Gita.

She saw Davy and Sarah. Davy and Sarah were playing with a skipping rope, and Mrs Pitter-Patter told them that they ought to play ball.

"And you shouldn't play in the lane," she said. "You should play in the garden of the old house, where you are in no one's way."

Mrs Pitter-Patter went on up the lane, and Davy and Sarah went on skipping in the lane.

She saw Mr Gotobed sitting outside
in the sunshine, and she told him
that he ought to be in bed.
Mrs Pitter-Patter went
on up the lane.
Mr Gotobed looked
at her and sighed.

He didn't say anything. He just
shut his eyes and dozed as he sat
in his chair in the sunshine.

Mrs Pitter-Patter came to the end of Puddle Lane. There was a very old house at the end of the lane, with gates leading into the garden. Mrs Pitter-Patter stopped at the gates. She looked into the garden.

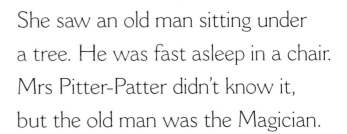

She saw an old man sitting under a tree. He was fast asleep in a chair. Mrs Pitter-Patter didn't know it, but the old man was the Magician.

Mrs Pitter-Patter opened the gate,
and went into the garden.
She went up to the Magician.
He was fast asleep.

"You shouldn't be fast asleep
at this time of day," she said.
"Wake up and do something!"

The Magician woke up.

He looked at Mrs Pitter-Patter.

"What do you want me to do?" he asked.

"Anything useful," said Mrs Pitter-Patter.

"Very well, I will," said the Magician.

"I'll do something very useful."

And he snapped his fingers.

The very next moment, Mrs Pitter-Patter
found herself getting smaller.

"Oh dear, oh dear!" cried Mrs Pitter-Patter.
"You're turning into a giant!
Help! Help! You're a giant!"

"I'm not growing bigger, but you're
growing smaller," said the Magician.

Mrs Pitter-Patter was so small by this
time that the Magician had to pick
her up and hold her in his hand
so that he could talk to her.

"Put me down! Put me down!"
cried Mrs Pitter-Patter.

"If I put you down, will you
go away and not bother me?"
asked the Magician.

"I'll go away. I'll never come
back!" said Mrs Pitter-Patter
shaking her fist.

"That's a bargain!" said the Magician.
He put Mrs Pitter-Patter down on the grass
and she ran through the grass to the gate.

She went under the gate
and out into Puddle Lane
as fast as she could go.

But as soon as she was safely back
in Puddle Lane, Mrs Pitter-Patter
was herself again.
She could hardly believe it.

She was just as tall as
she had always been.

Mrs Pitter-Patter ran down the lane. She wanted to get home as fast as she could. She met Hari and Gita, and Davy and Sarah. They were all playing together in the lane.

"Play in the lane if you like," said Mrs Pitter-Patter, "but never, never, NEVER go into the Magician's garden, or into that old house!"

And she ran home as fast as she could to make herself a cup of tea.

Old Mr Gotobed

Old Mr Gotobed's house at the end of Puddle Lane. It had a roof made of red-brown tiles. There were cracks in the wall too, but Mr Gotobed lived there very happily.

One night it began
to rain. It rained and
it rained and it rained,
until all the puddles
in Puddle Lane
were full of water.

Then the wind began
to blow. The wind blew
and it blew and it blew,
and it whistled round the
houses in Puddle Lane.

The wind blew harder and harder. It blew under the tiles on the roof of Mr Gotobed's house. It blew some of the tiles off the roof and down into the lane. There was a hole in the roof where the tiles had been. The rain ran down the roof. It ran down into the hole. It came in through the hole, and dripped on to the floor of the attic.

Drip, drip, drip.

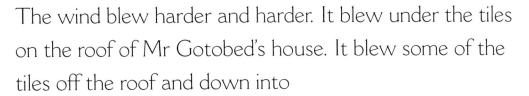

At seven o'clock in the morning,
old Mr Gotobed got up.

The rain was still raining and
the wind was still blowing.

So he didn't go out, and he
didn't see the hole in the roof.

At eight o'clock, old Mr Gotobed had his breakfast.

The rain was still raining and the wind was still blowing. Old Mr Gotobed still didn't go outside, so he didn't see the hole in the roof.

Old Mr Gotobed had dinner at eleven.
(He always felt hungry in the morning,
so he had dinner early.)

The rain was still raining and
the wind was still blowing.

Old Mr Gotobed still didn't
go out, so he still didn't see
the hole in the roof.

An hour later, the clock struck twelve.
It was noon. Old Mr Gotobed looked
at the clock. Then he looked out
of the window.

The rain was still raining and
the wind was still blowing.

"There's no place like bed when it's wet
and it's windy," said old Mr Gotobed.
And he went back to bed.

It was eight o'clock in the evening when at last the rain stopped. Mr Gotobed was still fast asleep in bed.

Up in the attic of Mr Gotobed's house, there was a very big puddle.

The rain had been coming in all day.

The wind blew the clouds away.
But the very big puddle was still
there in the attic. It was just
over Mr Gotobed's bed.
Three drops of water
dripped through a
crack in the ceiling.
They dripped onto
Mr Gotobed's toes.

Plop! Plop! Plop!

But Mr Gotobed
went on sleeping.

The water ran along the crack in the ceiling. Six drops of water dripped on to Mr Gotobed's knees.

Plop! Plop! Plop!
Plop! Plop! Plop!

But Mr Gotobed went on sleeping.

The moon came up over the roofs of the houses in Puddle Lane. The clouds had all blown away. But the water was still running along the crack in the ceiling. Nine drops of water dripped on to Mr Gotobed's nose.

Plop! Plop! Plop!
Plop! Plop! Plop!
Plop! Plop! Plop!

Mr Gotobed woke up.
He saw the moon shining in at
the window. He was just going
to get up, when the water
in the attic reached a hole
in the ceiling.

All the water that was left
in the attic fell through on
to Mr Gotobed's head in
one big swoosh!

"Ouch!" cried Mr Gotobed.

Poor Mr Gotobed! He was very wet.
It was midnight, too.

He got out of bed and put
on some warm, dry clothes.
Then he climbed up
a ladder into the attic
and saw the hole
in the roof.

Mr Gotobed shook his head.
"Oh dear! Oh dear!"
he said. "I shall have to do
something about that."

He looked around.
There was an old tin
bath in the roof.

Mr Gotobed pulled the bath
under the hole. He climbed
back down the ladder and
looked at his bed. His bed
was very wet.

Mr Gotobed shook his head.
He went downstairs.
He made up a bed by the fire,
sitting in his old armchair,
with his feet on the table.

By the time the moon
was high in the sky and
shining down into the lane,
old Mr Gotobed
was all tucked in,
asleep in his bed again.

Peter Puffle's Mouse

It was a fine day. The sun was shining down on Puddle Lane, and Davy and Sarah went out to play. They were just going into the garden at the end of the lane, when they saw Peter Puffle.

"Sarah! Davy! Wait for me!" shouted Peter Puffle.
He ran towards them.

Peter was carrying a little cage with a white mouse in it.

"Just look at her!" cried Peter, holding
up the cage. "Isn't she a beauty?
She's the best mouse you've ever seen!"

"Don't make such a noise,"
said Sarah. "You'll frighten her."

"Where did you get her?"
asked Davy.

"Uncle Percy gave her
to me," said Peter Puffle.
"Isn't she great?"

They went into the garden.

"I'm going to get some dry grass for my mouse," said Peter. "Then she can make a nest. Perhaps she'll have baby mice."

"We've got some nuts for the wood mice who live in the hollow tree," said Davy. "Come and see them."

"The wood mice can't be as good as my mouse," said Peter Puffle. "She's the best mouse in the town."

As they went towards the hollow tree they saw Mr Gotobed. Mr Gotobed was sitting on the grass, propped up against a stone bench. He was fast asleep, snoring gently.

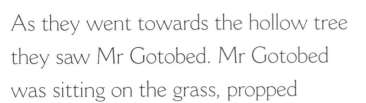

"What's he sleeping there for?" asked Peter.
"He's always sleeping," said Sarah.
"That's silly," said Peter.

They came to the hollow tree.

"This is where the wood mice live," said Sarah. "Have you got the nuts, Davy?"

Davy took a nut out of his pocket and dropped it into the hollow tree.

Peter peered in.
"I can't see any mice," he said.
"Shh!" said Sarah.
"You'll frighten them."

A wood mouse crept out of a hole in the tree, and began to eat the nut. "Look!" cried Peter. "There's one!"

The wood mouse picked up the nut and ran back down the hole as fast as he could. "You've frightened it away," said Sarah. "You have to be quiet, if you want to see wood mice."

"I'd rather have my mouse," said Peter. "She doesn't run away."

"She would if she could," said Sarah.

"No, she wouldn't!" said Peter. "Let's get the dry grass for her," said Davy.

There was some dry grass by the
hollow tree. Some of it was very
long. Davy and Peter picked
some handfuls of dry grass.

As they went back towards
the gates, they passed
Mr Gotobed. Mr Gotobed
was still fast asleep.
He was still snoring gently.

Peter put down the grass,
and the cage with the mouse
inside it. "Watch me!" he said.

He took a piece of long
grass and he tiptoed over to
Mr Gotobed. He began
to tickle Mr. Gotobed's nose
with the end of the grass.

Mr Gotobed's nose twitched.
He brushed his hand across
his face, but he didn't open
his eyes.

Peter tickled Mr Gotobed's nose again.
Mr Gotobed shook his head, but he
didn't wake up. Peter went on tickling.
Mr Gotobed gave a great sneeze.
"Atishoo!"
He sneezed again. "Atishoo!"

He opened his eyes, and
sat up. Peter hid the grass
behind his back.

"Hello, Peter," said Mr Gotobed. "Are you playing in the garden? There are a lot of flies in here today. One of them keeps landing on my nose!"

Mr Gotobed shut his eyes and settled down to sleep again.

Mr Gotobed was just beginning to snore when Sarah called out, "Peter! Where's your mouse? She's not in the cage."

Peter ran over to the cage.
The cage was empty.
The door was open
and the mouse had gone.

"You let it out!" said Peter.
"I didn't," said Sarah.
"You must have knocked
the catch off the door, when
you put the cage down,"
said Davy.

Peter began to cry.
"I've got to find her!" he said.
"I've got to!"

"We'll help you," said Davy.
"She can't have gone far."
"But you'll have to keep quiet,
Peter, or you'll frighten her,"
said Sarah.
Peter didn't answer.

They began to look for the mouse.
"What's that?" whispered Davy. "Look – over there in the grass." They crept over to look, but it wasn't the mouse. It was a frog.
"Where's it going?" whispered Davy, watching the frog.

"There's a lake on the other side of the house," whispered Sarah.
"Perhaps it's going there."

"We've got to find my mouse," said Peter tearfully.
"Don't go looking at frogs!"

"Let's look along the wall," said Sarah.
"There are some holes there.
Perhaps she's gone into one."

There were some snails on
the wall, but there was
no sign of the mouse.

"She's not here," said Peter,
"and I've got to find her. She must be somewhere."
"Perhaps she's with the wood mice," said Davy.
"I expect she was lonely, all on her own."
"No she wasn't," said Peter, "I played with her."

" Let's go back to the tree
and make sure she's not there,"
said Davy.

They were just going
back to the hollow tree
when Sarah whispered,
"Look!"

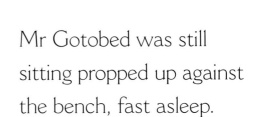

Mr Gotobed was still
sitting propped up against
the bench, fast asleep.

His hat was tilted over his eyes, and Peter's mouse was sitting on top of his hat! Peter was going to run forward but Sarah caught his arm.

"Sh!" she said. "Don't frighten her. Let Davy do it. He's good with mice."
Peter stopped.

Davy tiptoed over to Mr Gotobed.
He held out his hand and reached
out to Mr Gotobed's hat.

A nut was lying on his fingers.
The little mouse saw the nut.

Davy put his hand very close
to the hat, and the little mouse
climbed onto his hand
to eat the nut.

Davy gently carried the mouse
back to Peter.

"Here you are, Peter,"
he said.

"Let's put her back in
the cage," said Peter.
He opened the cage door.

"It's a very small cage for
a mouse," said Sarah.

"Uncle Percy's getting me
a bigger one," said Peter.
"He said he would, when
he gave her to me."

They had just put the little
mouse back in the cage,
when Mr Puffle came
into the garden.

"Hello, Sarah, Davy.
Has Peter been showing
you his mouse?" said Mr Puffle.
"Have you got the dry
grass, Peter?"

"I've got lots of it," said Peter.
"She can make a lovely warm
bed with all this."

"Good," said Mr Puffle. "I've got a much bigger cage for your mouse. And I've got another mouse, to be with her, so that she won't be lonely. Bring the mouse along and we'll put her in her new home."

So Sarah, Davy, Peter and the mouse all went back into Puddle Lane, to put Peter's mouse in her new home.

Puddle Lane is a strange street. Lots of unusual grown-ups live there as well as a group of children - and some magical little animals. But the strangest inhabitant by far is the Magician. After all, his magic spells can turn everyone's lives upside down!

You can read more stories about the people and animals that live in Puddle Lane
in:
The Wideawake Mice
The Wideawake Mice in Danger
The Magic Griffle